FUNDOO
T-SHIRT
QUOTES

Times
Group
Books
BOOKS AS MEDIA

Fundoo T-Shirt Quotes
Copyright © Bennett, Coleman & Co., Ltd. 2007.

First published in 2007

by

Bennett, Coleman & Co., Ltd.
7, Bahadur Shah Zafar Marg
New Delhi-110002

Compiled by	:	Soma B. Chowdhury
Cover & Design	:	Subhasish Munshi
Layout	:	Jitender Kumar
Printed and bound by	:	Batra Art Press

ISBN 978-81-89906-05-4
Price   :   Rs 95

Are you the type who loves to flaunt oodles of attitude all the time? Do you like to express yourself in short witty anecdotes? If you do, this book will serve as a ready reckoner for you. Fundoo T-Shirt Quotes will arm you with quotable quotes you can use in different circumstances. You can get the quotes printed on your outfit or tattooed on your body. If you like, you can use them in your conversation or in the written word to wriggle out of difficult situations and to appear witty and confident. Either way, the quotations can act as excellent substitutes for wit and enable you to attract attention.

The best part is that when you pour over these quotes, they might actually stimulate creative thinking and teach you to appreciate the fun element even in mundane events. While some of these are plain funny, others are ironic and thought provoking. The length of the quotes have been kept brief to enable easy assimilation and reflection.

Aimed at both young and old individuals, this compilation is for personal use as well as gifting purposes. It has over 300 quotes. So go ahead and give yourself a certain air with the weapon of wit.

Reality keeps
on ruining my
life

If you can't
take the heat,
don't tickle
the dragon

Don't judge me
based on your
ignorance

I wear the
brains in
the family

Nice person…
wrong planet

If you could read
my mind you
wouldn't be
smiling

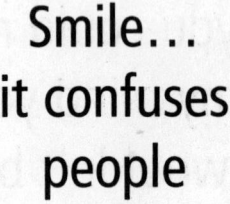

Smile…
it confuses
people

I'm usually slim
and gorgeous,
but it's my
day off!

You cannot
have
everything.
Where would
you put it?

Monday is an
awful way to
spend 1/7th of
your life

Who stopped
payment on my
reality check?

Puns are bad,
but poetry
is verse

A single fact can spoil a good argument

Take my advice,
I don't use
it anyway

The weather
is here, wish
you were
beautiful

I had a life
once…now
I have a
computer

Eat right,
stay fit,
die anyway

Smooth seas
never made a
good sailor

Bad is never
good until worse
happens

Money talks
but all mine
ever says is
"goodbye"

I get enough
exercise just
pushing my luck

Quoting one
is plagiarism.
Quoting many
is research

When I am
punctual,
nobody's
there to
appreciate it

Sorry, I don't
date outside
my species

I have nothing
to declare
except my
genius

It's not enough
to aim, you
must hit

All true
wisdom
is found on
t-shirts

It's been
Monday all
week

In the
middle of
middle of
difficulty lies
opportunity

If you can't see
the bright side
of life, polish
the dull side

Moderation is
a fatal thing.
Nothing
succeeds like
excess

I'll conquer my
procrastination
problem.
JUST YOU WAIT!

No one listens
to me until
I make a
mistake

After all is
said and done,
usually more is
said than done

Conscience is
what hurts
when
everything else
feels good

Egotism: Doing
a crossword
puzzle with
a pen

Every silver
lining has
a cloud
around it

Justice: A
decision in
your favour

Talk is cheap
because supply
exceeds demand

I don't get
even, I just
get more odd

Cleverly
disguised as
a responsible
adult

If you are
rich…I am
single

If something's
hard to do then
it's not worth
doing

Don't interrupt
me when I am
talking to myself

Happy?
Don't worry, you
will get over it

As I said
before,
I NEVER
repeat myself

Baby philosophy - If it stinks, change it

A single fact can
spoil a good
argument

If you don't
like my
opinion of you
— Improve
yourself!

If ignorance is bliss, why aren't more people happy?

A pessimist is
an optimist with
experience

If you need
space, join
NASA

Most people deserve each other

Sorry if I look
interested!
I'm not!

If your dog
doesn't like
anyone, you
probably
shouldn't
either

Wit is educated
insolence

They spoil
every romance
by trying to
make it last
forever

Heaven doesn't
want me.
Hell is afraid
I'll take over

Be yourself:
everyone else
is already taken

How much can
I get away with
and still go
to heaven?

Just when I
find the keys
to success,
someone
changes all
the locks

I am not
selfish…
I just want
everything!

I love
attention…
Just not
from you

I am always
satisfied with
the best

I'm not as
think as you
drunk I am

Artist seeks boss
with vision
impairment

Boys will be boys, and so will a lot of middle-aged men

Despite the high cost of living, it remains popular

Don't you hate
it when life
doesn't follow
the manuals?

I just wish my
mouth had a
backspace key

Know thyself —
but don't tell
anyone

Laugh at your
problems;
everyone
else does

Love means
nothing to a
tennis player

My job is secure.
No one else
wants it

Love is grand;
divorce is
a hundred
grand

To err is human.
To admit it is
a blunder

I put the fun in
dysfunctional

Lead me not into temptation. I can find it myself

Too many freaks,
not enough
circuses

I'm the person
your mother
warned you
about

I'm modest
and proud
of it

The fact that no one understands you, doesn't mean you're an artist

Everyone is
entitled to
my opinion

I don't suffer
from stress.
I am a carrier

When everything's coming your way, you are in the wrong lane

Love your
neighbour,
but don't get
caught

The voices in
my head are
telling me I
don't like you

I'm not totally useless! I can be used as a bad example

Don't drink
and drive…
you might go
over a bump
and spill your
drink!

Your future
depends on your
dreams — So
go to sleep!

We always hold hands. If I let go, she shops

If wishes were
horses, I'd own
a stud farm
by now

Few women
admit their
age. Few men
act theirs

Where there is a
will, there are
500 relatives

Ladies first.
Pretty ladies
sooner

I'd like to help
you out; which
way did you
come in?

Artificial
intelligence is
no match for
natural stupidity

I refuse to have
a battle of
wits with
an unarmed
opponent

The difference between in-laws and outlaws? Outlaws are wanted

Success is a
relative term —
it brings so
many relatives

There are two
kinds of
pedestrians:
the quick and
the dead

It's not hard
to meet
expenses,
they're
everywhere

It is not
enough to
succeed.
Others must
fail in the
process

The men
without money
are after our
money

My favourite
mythical
creature?
The honest
politician

A conclusion
is what you
reach when
you get tired
of thinking

Borrow
money from a
pessimist —
they don't
expect
it back

Classic: a book which people praise, but don't read

Logic will get
you from A to
B. Imagination
will take you
everywhere

On the keyboard
of life, always
keep one
finger on the
escape key

When you are right, no one remembers. When you are wrong, no one forgets

There are 3 sides to any argument: yours, mine & the right side

Hard work will
pay off later.
Laziness pays
off now!

If you can't change your mind, are you sure you still have one?

Marriage is
give and take.
You better give
it to her or
she'll take it
anyway

Work fascinates
me. I can look
at it for hours!

It's not an
attitude. It's
the way
I am!

Better to
understand a
little than to
misunderstand
a lot

I used to have
an open mind
but my brains
kept falling
out

You can't buy
love. But you
pay heavily
for it

I think,
therefore
I'm single

Good girls are
bad girls
that never get
caught

Saving is the best thing. Especially when your parents have done it for you

I'm not cynical.
I'm just
experienced

Age is a very
high price
to pay for
maturity

Never make the
same mistake
twice. There are
so many new
ones to make

I don't have
an attitude.
I have a
personality
you can't
handle

Nice perfume.
Must you
marinate
in it?

Sarcasm is
just one
more service
I offer

Don't hate yourself in the morning. Sleep till noon

Anyone going slower than you is an idiot. Anyone going faster is a maniac

By the time
you can make
ends meet, they
move the ends

A clear
conscience is
usually the
sign of a bad
memory

Of all the things I've lost, I miss my mind the most

There is an
angel inside
me whom I
am constantly
shocking

This isn't an
office. It's hell
with fluorescent
lighting

Stupidity is not a crime, so you are free to go!

The trouble with
real life is that
there is no
danger music

See no evil,
hear no evil,
date no evil

Nothing in
the world is
more dangerous
than sincere
ignorance and
conscientious
stupidity

Aim for the stars. But first, aim for their bodyguards

If no one
understand you,
doesn't mean
you're an artist

I'm not
anti-social.
Society is
anti me

There's never a
wrong time to
do the right
thing

Our life is
simply what
our thoughts
make it!

Experience is
like a comb.
You get it when
you're bald!

The shell might break before the bird can fly!

A ship in the harbour is safe. But that's not why they are built!

This is an
excellent time
for you to
become a
missing person

You're a habit
I'd like to
kick — with
both feet.

You laugh at me 'coz I'm different. I laugh at you 'coz you're all the same

Leadership is
action, not
position

I hear you are
connected to
the Police
Department —
by a pair of
handcuffs

Wrinkled was not one of the things I wanted to be when I grew up

Born to party,
forced to work!

I don't have a license to kill. I have a learner's permit

Leadership is
doing what is
right when
no one is
watching

If man could
create a perfect
woman, he'd
probably cheat
on her

Join the army, visit exotic places, meet strange people, then kill them

I could kill for
a noble peace
prize

Many people
quit looking for
work when they
find a job

I couldn't repair
your brakes, so
I made your
horn louder

If everything
seems to be
going well,
you have
obviously
overlooked
something

What is popular
is not always
right and what
is right is not
always popular

When I'm in
my right mind,
my left mind
gets pretty
crowded

Sometimes 'the majority' only means that all the fools are on the same side

I was born
intelligent,
education
spoilt me

I lied to get the
job, they lied
about the job.
We're even

I am a bomb technician. If you see me running, try to keep up

There cannot be
a crisis today.
My schedule is
already full

I'm not getting
smaller. I'm
backing away
from you

Alcohol and calculus don't mix. Never drink and derive

Humour is
just another
defense
against the
universe

Hug me for
best results

Budget: A method for going broke methodically

If things get any
worse, I'll have
to ask you to
stop helping me

If at first you
do succeed, try
not to look
astonished!

Loves takes
up where
knowledge
leaves off

Forgive many
things in
others, nothing
in yourself

There is no
revenge so
complete as
forgiveness

The only way to
have a friend
is to be one

Nothing will
work unless
you do it

Every noble
work is at first
impossible

Write angry
letters to your
enemies. Never
mail them

Men always
want to be
right

Never mistake
motion for
action

Humour is
mankind's
greatest
blessing

The art of living
is more like
wrestling than
dancing

Love is the beauty of the soul

A philosopher
always knows
what to do
until it happens
to him

Inflexibility is
the hallmark of
the tiny mind

A good marriage
would be
between a blind
wife and a deaf
husband

Worrying works! 90% of the things I worry about never happen

Crime doesn't pay...Does that mean my job is a crime?

The secret to
success is
knowing who
to blame for
your failures

Those who trim
themselves to
suit everybody
will soon whittle
themselves
away

It's no
accident that
stressed
spelled
backwards
is desserts

The greatest
lesson in life is
to know that
even fools are
right sometimes

Don't wish
it was easier,
wish you were
better

What the superior man seeks is in himself; what the small man seeks is in others

I can't
remember if
I'm the good
twin or the
evil one

Chaos, panic
and disorder.
My work here
is done

I'm not tense,
just terribly
terribly alert

Smile, it's the
best thing you
can do with
your lips

Whatever kind
of look you were
going for, you
missed

Punctuality is
the virtue of
the bored

The best
things in life
are for free. So
stop working

Nothing succeeds like excess

Strangers have
the best candy

Life is too important to be taken seriously

I don't want
to earn my
living; I want
to live

There is no
sincerer love
than the love
of food

Why be
difficult
when you can
be impossible?

What happens
if you get scared
half to death
twice?

I'm sorry, but you looked better from far away

School prepares
you for the real
world which is
equally bad

Mental floss
prevents moral
decay

Facts are
stubborn
things

I've a firm grip on reality. Now I can strangle it

Typos? Blame
my cat

I used up all
my sick days,
so I called
in dead

I'm not only
weird. I'm
gifted too

You never
know what
you know!

Beat the 5 o'clock rush — Leave work at noon

If you don't
like the news,
go and make
some

How can I
miss you if
you won't
go away?

I'm one of those bad things that happen to good people

Every time you
open your
mouth, some
idiot starts
talking

I know Karate,
Kung Fu and
47 other
dangerous
words

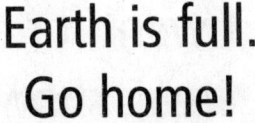

Earth is full.
Go home!

I went for a freak show and they let me in for nothing

It's hard to be
nostalgic if you
can't remember
anything

Don't treat me
any differently
than you
would the
queen

We are all in the gutter, but some of us are looking at the stars

Guys have
feelings too.
But, like…
who cares?

Treat each day
as your last,
one day you
will be right

Two wrongs
are only the
beginning

I can handle
pain until it
hurts

Humpty Dumpty
was pushed

Ask me about
my vow of
silence

How does a bulb
know when
it has an
idea?

You have the
right to remain
silent, so please
SHUT UP

I'll try being nicer when you try being smarter

Do NOT start
with me. You
will NOT win

In the middle of
difficulty lies
opportunity

Looking good
is a curse

The days of the
digital watch
are numbered

Stop reading
my shirt

Every woman
is a rebel, and
usually in wild
revolt against
herself

My wife and
I were happy
for 20 years.
Then we met

Never answer
an anonymous
letter

I didn't say it
was your fault.
I said I was
blaming you

Teach me the rules…and I'll teach you how to break them

Ability is what gets you to the top if the boss has no daughter

When you're
down and
out, drag
somebody else
with you

Lethal use
of farce

There is no 'me' in team. No, wait, yes there is!

Forgive your
enemies as
nothing annoys
them so much

I find it easier to fight for principles than to live up to them

All I ask is to
prove that
money can't
make me happy

A good pun
is its own
reword

People say
nothing is
impossible, but I
do nothing
everyday

Anyone who
makes an
absolute
statement is
a fool

Can you think of
another word
for synonym?

Blessed are
the censors;
they shall
inhibit the
earth

Cloning is the
sincerest form
of flattery

Give a sceptic
an inch and
he'll measure it

Great minds
run in great
circles

How come
wrong numbers
are never busy?

Illiterate?
Write for
free help

Let's hope God
grades on a
curve

Knocked; you
weren't in —
Opportunity

Love thy
neighbour:
Tune thy piano

Never put off till tomorrow what you can ignore entirely

How is it possible to have a 'civil' war?

The chief cause
of problems are
solutions

The early worm
deserves the
bird

Two wrongs
don't make a
right, but three
lefts do

Why is 'abbreviated' such a long word?

All that glitters
has a high
refractive index

A little drama
never hurt
anyone

I'm not lazy, just motivationally challenged

As a matter of
fact, the world
does revolve
around me

Stupid people
make my
brain sad

I think, therefore
I can't sleep

99 per cent
angel

A day without
sunshine is
like night

Just who do
you think
I am?

I not only use all the brains that I have, but also all that I can borrow

If at first you
don't succeed,
destroy all
evidence that
you tried

Be unique and different, just say yes

Everyone needs
to believe in
something. I
believe in
chocolate

Everyone has
a photographic
memory. Some
don't have
a film

You are only as
good as your
last haircut

True friends
stab you in
the front

A hangover is
the wrath of
grapes

All men are idiots, and I married their king!

Time flies like an arrow. Fruit flies like a banana

One tequila two
tequila three
tequila floor

Live your life so
the preacher
won't have to
lie at your
funeral

The way to see
by faith is to
shut the eye
of reason

God, if you can't make me skinny, please make my friends fat!

Time is the best
teacher, but
it kills all its
students

The secret of
a successful
marriage is not
to be at home
too much

I'm not a
complete idiot.
Some parts are
still missing

I can't
remember
the last time
I forgot
something

What is a free gift? Aren't all gifts free?

Never mess
up an apology
with an excuse

Never test the
depth of water
with both feet

If you want
breakfast in
bed, sleep in
the kitchen

Coffee, chocolate, men…Some things are just better rich

He who laughs
last, thinks
slowest

You are
depriving
some village
of its idiot

I need not suffer
in silence when
I can still moan,
whimper and
complain

One good turn
gets most of
the blankets

Next time you
get the urge to
think...don't!

Good morning is
an oxymoron